At the Sign of the Cat and Racket

Fabulous Novellas

At the Sign of the Cat and Racket

(La Maison du chat-qui-pelote)

by
Honoré de Balzac

Translated by
Clara Bell

Skomlin
House of Memory

Skomlin
House of Memory and Imagination
For more information visit *www.skomlin.com*

A Skomlin Book
Melbourne, Australia

First published 1830
This translation published in 1895
© Skomlin, 2017

ISBN: 978-0-6482388-3-6 *(paperback)*
ISBN: 978-0-6482388-4-3   *(eBook)*

 A catalogue record for this book is available from the National Library of Australia

The paper used in this publication meets the minimum requirements of ANSI/NISO Z39.48-1992 (R1997) (Permanence of Paper). The paper used in this book is from responsibly managed forests. Printed in the United States of America, the United Kingdom and Australia by Lightning Source, Inc.

To Mademoiselle Marie de Montheau

AT THE SIGN OF THE CAT AND RACKET

Half-way down the Rue Saint-Denis, almost at the corner of the Rue du Petit-Lion, there stood formerly one of those delightful houses which enable historians to reconstruct old Paris by analogy. The threatening walls of this tumbledown abode seemed to have been decorated with hieroglyphics. For what other name could the passer-by give to the Xs and Vs which the horizontal or diagonal timbers traced on the front, outlined by little parallel cracks in the plaster? It was evident that every beam quivered in its mortices at the passing of the lightest vehicle. This venerable structure was crowned by a triangular roof of which no example will, ere long, be seen in Paris. This covering, warped by the extremes of the Paris climate, projected three feet over the roadway, as much to protect the threshold from the rainfall as to shelter the wall of a loft and its sill-less dormer-window. This upper story was built of planks, overlapping each other like slates, in order, no doubt, not to overweight the frail house.

One rainy morning in the month of March, a young man, carefully wrapped in his cloak, stood under the awning of a shop opposite this old house, which he was studying with the enthusiasm of an antiquary. In point of fact, this relic of the civic life of the sixteenth century offered more than one problem to the consideration of an observer. Each story presented some singularity; on the first floor four tall, narrow windows, close together, were filled as to the lower panes with boards, so as to produce the doubtful light by which a clever salesman can ascribe to his goods the color his customers inquire for. The young man seemed very scornful of this part of the house; his eyes had not yet rested on it. The windows of the second floor, where the Venetian blinds were drawn up, revealing little dingy muslin curtains behind the large Bohemian glass panes, did not interest him either. His attention was attracted to the third floor, to the modest sash-frames of wood, so clumsily wrought that they might have found a place in the Museum of Arts and Crafts to illustrate the early efforts of French carpentry. These windows were glazed with small squares of glass so green that, but for his good eyes, the young man could not have seen the blue-checked cotton curtains which screened the mysteries of the room from profane eyes. Now and then the watcher, weary of his fruitless contemplation, or of the silence in which the house was buried, like the whole neighborhood, dropped his eyes towards the lower regions. An involuntary smile parted his lips each time he looked at the shop, where, in fact, there were some laughable details.

A formidable wooden beam, resting on four pillars, which appeared to have bent under the weight of the decrepit house, had been encrusted with as many coats of different paint as there are of rouge on an old duchess' cheek. In the middle of this broad and fantastically carved joist there was an old painting representing a cat playing rackets. This picture was what moved the young man to mirth. But it must be said that the wittiest of modern painters could not invent so comical a caricature. The animal held in one of its forepaws a racket as big as itself, and stood on its hind legs to aim at hitting an enormous ball, returned by a man in a fine embroidered coat. Drawing, color, and accessories, all were treated in such a way as to suggest that the artist had meant to make game of the shop-owner and of the passing observer. Time, while impairing this artless painting, had made it yet more grotesque by introducing some uncertain features which must have puzzled the conscientious idler. For instance, the cat's tail had been eaten into in such a way that it might now have been taken for the figure of a spectator—so long, and thick, and furry were the tails of our forefathers' cats. To the right of the picture, on an azure field which ill-disguised the decay of the wood, might be read the name "Guillaume," and to the left, "Successor to Master Chevrel." Sun and rain had worn away most of the gilding parsimoniously applied to the letters of this superscription, in which the Us and Vs had changed places in obedience to the laws of old-world orthography.

To quench the pride of those who believe that the world is growing cleverer day by day, and that modern humbug surpasses everything, it may be observed that these signs, of which the origin seems so whimsical to many Paris merchants, are the dead pictures of once living pictures by which our roguish ancestors contrived to tempt customers into their houses. Thus the Spinning Sow, the Green Monkey, and others, were animals in cages whose skills astonished the passer-by, and whose accomplishments prove the patience of the fifteenth-century artisan. Such curiosities did more to enrich their fortunate owners than the signs of "Providence," "Goodfaith," "Grace of God," and "Decapitation of John the Baptist," which may still be seen in the Rue Saint Denis.

However, our stranger was certainly not standing there to admire the cat, which a minute's attention sufficed to stamp on his memory. The young man himself had his peculiarities. His cloak, folded after the manner of an antique drapery, showed a smart pair of shoes, all the more remarkable in the midst of the Paris mud, because he wore white silk stockings, on which the splashes betrayed his impatience. He had just come, no doubt, from a wedding or a ball; for at this early hour he had in his hand a pair of white gloves, and his black hair, now out of curl, and flowing over his shoulders, showed that it had been dressed a la Caracalla, a fashion introduced as much by David's school of painting as by the mania for Greek and Roman styles which characterized the early years of this century.

In spite of the noise made by a few market garden-

3

ers, who, being late, rattled past towards the great market-place at a gallop, the busy street lay in a stillness of which the magic charm is known only to those who have wandered through deserted Paris at the hours when its roar, hushed for a moment, rises and spreads in the distance like the great voice of the sea. This strange young man must have seemed as curious to the shopkeeping folk of the "Cat and Racket" as the "Cat and Racket" was to him. A dazzlingly white cravat made his anxious face look even paler than it really was. The fire that flashed in his black eyes, gloomy and sparkling by turns, was in harmony with the singular outline of his features, with his wide, flexible mouth, hardened into a smile. His forehead, knit with violent annoyance, had a stamp of doom. Is not the forehead the most prophetic feature of a man? When the stranger's brow expressed passion the furrows formed in it were terrible in their strength and energy; but when he recovered his calmness, so easily upset, it beamed with a luminous grace which gave great attractiveness to a countenance in which joy, grief, love, anger, or scorn blazed out so contagiously that the coldest man could not fail to be impressed.

He was so thoroughly vexed by the time when the dormer-window of the loft was suddenly flung open, that he did not observe the apparition of three laughing faces, pink and white and chubby, but as vulgar as the face of Commerce as it is seen in sculpture on certain monuments. These three faces, framed by the window, recalled the puffy cherubs floating among the clouds that surround God the Father. The apprentices snuffed up the exhalations of the street with an eagerness that showed how hot and poisonous the atmosphere of their garret must be. After pointing to the singular sentinel, the most jovial, as he seemed, of the apprentices retired and came back holding an instrument whose hard metal pipe is now superseded by a leather tube; and they all grinned with mischief as they looked down on the loiterer, and sprinkled him with a fine white shower of which the scent proved that three chins had just been shaved. Standing on tiptoe, in the farthest corner of their loft, to enjoy their victim's rage, the lads ceased laughing on seeing the haughty indifference with which the young man shook his cloak, and the intense contempt expressed by his face as he glanced up at the empty window-frame.

At this moment a slender white hand threw up the lower half of one of the clumsy windows on the third floor by the aid of the sash runners, of which the pulley so often suddenly gives way and releases the heavy panes it ought to hold up. The watcher was then rewarded for his long waiting. The face of a young girl appeared, as fresh as one of the white cups that bloom on the bosom of the waters, crowned by a frill of tumbled muslin, which gave her head a look of exquisite innocence. Though wrapped in brown stuff, her neck and shoulders gleamed here and there through little openings left by her movements in sleep. No expression of embarrassment detracted from the candor of her face, or the calm look of eyes immortalized long since in the sublime works of Raphael; here were the same grace, the same repose as in those Virgins, and now proverbial. There was a delightful contrast between the cheeks of that face on which sleep had, as it were, given high relief to a superabundance of life, and the antiquity of the heavy window with its clumsy shape and black sill. Like those day-blowing flowers, which in the early morning have not yet unfurled their cups, twisted by the chills of night, the girl, as yet hardly awake, let her blue eyes wander beyond the neighboring roofs to look at the sky; then, from habit, she cast them down on the gloomy depths of the street, where they immediately met those of her adorer. Vanity, no doubt, distressed her at being seen in undress; she started back, the worn pulley gave way, and the sash fell with the rapid run, which in our day has earned for this artless invention of our forefathers an odious name, Fenetre a la Guillotine. The vision had disappeared. To the young man the most radiant star of morning seemed to be hidden by a cloud.

During these little incidents the heavy inside shutters that protected the slight windows of the shop of the "Cat and Racket" had been removed as if by magic. The old door with its knocker was opened back against the wall of the entry by a man-servant, apparently coeval with the sign, who, with a shaking hand, hung upon it a square of cloth, on which were embroidered in yellow silk the words: "Guillaume, successor to Chevrel." Many a passer-by would have found it difficult to guess the class of trade carried on by Monsieur Guillaume. Between the strong iron bars which protected his shop windows on the outside, certain packages, wrapped in brown linen, were hardly visible, though as numerous as herrings swimming in a shoal. Notwithstanding the primitive aspect of the Gothic front, Monsieur Guillaume, of all the merchant clothiers in Paris, was the one whose stores were always the best provided, whose connections were the most extensive, and whose commercial honesty never lay under the slightest suspicion. If some of his brethren in business made a contract with the Government, and had not the required quantity of cloth, he was always ready to deliver it, however large the number of pieces tendered for. The wily dealer knew a thousand ways of extracting the largest profits without being obliged, like them, to court patrons, cringing to them, or making them costly presents. When his fellow-tradesmen could only pay in good bills of long date, he would mention his notary as an accommodating man, and managed to get a second profit out of the bargain, thanks to this arrangement, which had made it a proverb among the traders of the Rue Saint-Denis: "Heaven preserve you from Monsieur Guillaume's notary!" to signify a heavy discount.

The old merchant was to be seen standing on the threshold of his shop, as if by a miracle, the instant the servant withdrew. Monsieur Guillaume looked at the Rue Saint-Denis, at the neighboring shops, and at the weather, like a man disembarking at Havre, and seeing France once more after a long voyage. Having convinced himself that nothing had changed while he was asleep, he presently perceived the stranger on guard, and he, on his part, gazed at the patriarchal draper as Humboldt may have scrutinized the first electric eel he saw in America. Monsieur Guillaume wore loose black velvet breeches, pepper-and-salt stockings, and square toed shoes with silver buckles. His coat, with square-cut fronts, square-cut tails, and square-cut collar clothed his slightly bent figure in greenish cloth, finished with white metal buttons, tawny from wear. His gray hair was so accurately combed and flattened over his yellow pate that it made it look like a furrowed field. His little green eyes, that might have been pierced with a gimlet, flashed beneath arches faintly tinged with red in the place of eyebrows. Anxieties had wrinkled his forehead with as many horizontal lines as there were creases in his coat. This colorless face expressed patience, commercial shrewdness, and the sort of wily cupidity which is needful in business. At that time these old families were less rare than they are now, in which the characteristic habits and costume of their calling, surviving in the midst of more recent civilization, were preserved as cherished traditions, like the antediluvian remains found by Cuvier in the quarries.

The head of the Guillaume family was a notable upholder of ancient practices; he might be heard to regret the Provost of Merchants, and never did he mention a decision of the Tribunal of Commerce without calling it the Sentence of the Consuls. Up and dressed the first of the household, in obedience, no doubt, to these old customs, he stood sternly awaiting the appearance of his three assistants, ready to scold them in case they were late. These young disciples of Mercury knew nothing more terrible than the wordless assiduity with which the master scrutinized their faces and their movements on Monday in search of evidence or traces of their pranks. But at this moment the old clothier paid no heed to his apprentices; he was absorbed in trying to divine the motive of the anxious looks which the young man in silk stockings and a cloak cast alternately at his signboard and into the depths of his shop. The daylight was now brighter, and enabled the stranger to discern the cashier's corner enclosed by a railing and screened by old green silk curtains, where were kept the immense ledgers, the silent oracles of the house. The too inquisitive gazer seemed to covet this little nook, and to be taking the plan of a dining-room at one side, lighted by a skylight, whence the family at meals could easily see the smallest incident that might occur at the shop-door. So much affection for his dwelling seemed suspicious to a trader who had lived long enough to remember the law of maximum prices; Monsieur Guillaume naturally thought that this sinister personage had an eye to the till of the Cat and Racket. After quietly observing the mute duel which was going on between his master and the stranger, the eldest of the apprentices, having seen that the young man was stealthily watching the windows of the third floor, ventured to place himself on the stone flag where Monsieur Guillaume was standing. He took two steps out into the street, raised his head, and fancied that he caught sight of Mademoiselle Augustine Guillaume in hasty retreat. The draper, annoyed by his assistant's perspicacity, shot a side glance at him; but the draper and his amorous apprentice were suddenly relieved from the fears which the young man's presence had excited in their minds. He hailed a hackney cab on its way to a neighboring stand, and jumped into it with an air of affected indifference. This departure was a balm to the hearts of the other two lads, who had been somewhat uneasy as to meeting the victim of their practical joke.

"Well, gentlemen, what ails you that you are standing there with your arms folded?" said Monsieur Guillaume to his three neophytes. "In former days, bless you, when I was in Master Chevrel's service, I should have over-hauled more than two pieces of cloth by this time."

"Then it was daylight earlier," said the second assistant, whose duty this was.

The old shopkeeper could not help smiling. Though two of these young fellows, who were confided to his care by their fathers, rich manufacturers at Louviers and at Sedan, had only to ask and to have a hundred thousand francs the day when they were old enough to settle in life, Guillaume regarded it as his duty to keep them under the rod of an old-world despotism, unknown now-adays in the showy modern shops, where the apprentices expect to be rich men at thirty. He made them work like Negroes. These three assistants were equal to a business which would harry ten such clerks as those whose sybaritical tastes now swell the columns of the budget. Not a sound disturbed the peace of this solemn house, where the hinges were always oiled, and where the meanest article of furniture showed the respectable cleanliness which reveals strict order and economy. The most waggish of the three youths often amused him-self by writing the date of its first appearance on the Gruyere cheese which was left to their tender mercies at breakfast, and which it was their pleasure to leave untouched. This bit of mischief, and a few others of the same stamp, would sometimes bring a smile on the face of the younger of Guillaume's daughters, the pretty maiden who has just now appeared to the bewitched man in the street.

Though each of these apprentices, even the eldest, paid a round sum for his board, not one of them would have been bold enough to remain at the master's table when dessert was served. When Madame Guillaume talked of dressing the salad, the hapless youths trembled as they thought of the thrift with which her prudent hand dispensed the oil. They could never think of spending a night away from the house without having given, long before, a plausible reason for such an irregularity. Every Sunday, each in his turn, two of them accompanied the Guillaume family to Mass at Saint-Leu, and to vespers. Mesdemoiselles Virginie and Augustine, simply attired in cotton print, each took the arm of an apprentice and walked in front, under the piercing eye of their mother, who closed the little family procession with her husband, accustomed by her to carry two large prayer-books, bound in black morocco. The second apprentice received no salary. As for the eldest, whose twelve years of perseverance and discretion had initiated him into the secrets of the house, he was paid eight hundred francs a year as the reward of his labors. On certain family festivals he received as a gratuity some little gift, to which Madame Guillaume's dry and wrinkled hand alone gave value—netted purses, which she took care to stuff with cotton wool, to show off the fancy stitches, braces of the strongest make, or heavy silk stockings. Sometimes, but rarely, this prime minister was admitted to share the pleasures of the family when they went into the country, or when, after waiting for months, they made up their mind to exert the right acquired by taking a box at the theatre to command a piece which Paris had already forgotten.

As to the other assistants, the barrier of respect which formerly divided a master draper from his apprentices was that they would have been more likely to steal a piece of cloth than to infringe this time-honored etiquette. Such reserve may now appear ridiculous; but these old houses were a school of honesty and sound morals. The masters adopted their apprentices. The young man's linen was cared for, mended, and often replaced by the mistress of the house. If an apprentice fell ill, he was the object of truly maternal attention. In a case of danger the master lavished his money in calling in the most celebrated physicians, for he was not answerable to their parents merely for the good conduct and training of the lads. If one of them, whose character was unimpeachable, suffered misfortune, these old tradesmen knew how to value the intelligence he had displayed, and they did not hesitate to entrust the happiness of their daughters to men whom they had long trusted with their fortunes. Guillaume was one of these men of the old school, and if he had their ridiculous side, he had all their good qualities; and Joseph Lebas, the chief assistant, an orphan without any fortune, was in his mind destined to be the husband of Virginie, his elder daughter. But Joseph did not share the symmetrical ideas of his master, who would not for an empire have given his second daughter in marriage before the elder. The unhappy assistant felt that his heart was wholly given to Mademoiselle Augustine, the younger. In order to justify this passion, which had grown up in secret, it is necessary to inquire a little further into the springs of the absolute government which ruled the old cloth-merchant's household.

Guillaume had two daughters. The elder, Mademoiselle Virginie, was the very image of her mother. Madame Guillaume, daughter of the Sieur Chevrel, sat so upright in the stool behind her desk, that more than once she had heard some wag bet that she was a stuffed figure. Her long, thin face betrayed exaggerated piety. Devoid of attractions or of amiable manners, Madame Guillaume commonly decorated her head—that of a woman near on sixty—with a cap of a particular and unvarying shape, with long lappets, like that of a widow. In all the neighborhood she was known as the "portress nun." Her speech was curt, and her movements had the stiff precision of a semaphore. Her eye, with a gleam in it like a cat's, seemed to spite the world because she was so ugly. Mademoiselle Virginie, brought up, like her younger sister, under the domestic rule of her mother, had reached the age of eight-and-twenty. Youth mitigated the graceless effect which her likeness to her mother sometimes gave to her features, but maternal austerity had endowed her with two great qualities which made up for everything. She was patient and gentle. Mademoiselle Augustine, who was but just eighteen, was not like either her father or her mother. She was one of those daughters whose total absence of any physical affinity with their parents makes one believe in the adage: "God gives children." Augustine was little, or, to describe her more truly, delicately made. Full of gracious candor, a man of the world could have found no fault in the charming girl beyond a certain meanness of gesture or vulgarity of attitude, and sometimes a want of ease. Her silent and placid face was full of the transient melancholy which comes over all young girls who are too weak to dare to resist their mother's will.

The two sisters, always plainly dressed, could not gratify the innate vanity of womanhood but by a luxury of cleanliness which became them wonderfully, and made them harmonize with the polished counters and the shining shelves, on which the old man-servant never left a speck of dust, and with the old-world simplicity of all they saw about them. As their style of living compelled them to find the elements of happiness in persistent work, Augustine and Virginie had hitherto always satisfied their mother, who secretly prided herself on the perfect characters of her two daughters. It is easy to imagine the results of the training they had received. Brought up to a commercial life, accustomed to hear nothing but dreary arguments and calculations about trade, having studied nothing but grammar, book-keeping, a little Bible-history, and the history of France in

Le Ragois, and never reading any book but what their mother would sanction, their ideas had not acquired much scope. They knew perfectly how to keep house; they were familiar with the prices of things; they understood the difficulty of amassing money; they were economical, and had a great respect for the qualities that make a man of business. Although their father was rich, they were as skilled in darning as in embroidery; their mother often talked of having them taught to cook, so that they might know how to order a dinner and scold a cook with due knowledge. They knew nothing of the pleasures of the world; and, seeing how their parents spent their exemplary lives, they very rarely suffered their eyes to wander beyond the walls of their hereditary home, which to their mother was the whole universe. The meetings to which family anniversaries gave rise filled in the future of earthly joy to them.

When the great drawing-room on the second floor was to be prepared to receive company—Madame Roguin, a Demoiselle Chevrel, fifteen months younger than her cousin, and bedecked with diamonds; young Rabourdin, employed in the Finance Office; Monsieur Cesar Birotteau, the rich perfumer, and his wife, known as Madame Cesar; Monsieur Camusot, the richest silk mercer in the Rue des Bourdonnais, with his father-in-law, Monsieur Cardot, two or three old bankers, and some immaculate ladies—the arrangements, made necessary by the way in which everything was packed away—the plate, the Dresden china, the candlesticks, and the glass—made a variety in the monotonous lives of the three women, who came and went and exerted themselves as nuns would to receive their bishop. Then, in the evening, when all three were tired out with having wiped, rubbed, unpacked, and arranged all the gauds of the festival, as the girls helped their mother to undress, Madame Guillaume would say to them, "Children, we have done nothing today."

When, on very great occasions, "the portress nun" allowed dancing, restricting the games of boston, whist, and backgammon within the limits of her bedroom, such a concession was accounted as the most unhoped felicity, and made them happier than going to the great balls, to two or three of which Guillaume would take the girls at the time of the Carnival.

And once a year the worthy draper gave an entertainment, when he spared no expense. However rich and fashionable the persons invited might be, they were careful not to be absent; for the most important houses on the exchange had recourse to the immense credit, the fortune, or the time-honored experience of Monsieur Guillaume. Still, the excellent merchant's daughters did not benefit as much as might be supposed by the lessons the world has to offer to young spirits. At these parties, which were indeed set down in the ledger to the credit of the house, they wore dresses the shabbiness of which made them blush. Their style of dancing was not in any way remarkable, and their mother's surveillance did not allow of their holding any conversation with their partners beyond Yes and No. Also, the law of the old sign of the Cat and Racket commanded that they should be home by eleven o'clock, the hour when balls and fetes begin to be lively. Thus their pleasures, which seemed to conform very fairly to their father's position, were often made insipid by circumstances which were part of the family habits and principles.

As to their usual life, one remark will sufficiently paint it. Madame Guillaume required her daughters to be dressed very early in the morning, to come down every day at the same hour, and she ordered their employments with monastic regularity. Augustine, however, had been gifted by chance with a spirit lofty enough to feel the emptiness of such a life. Her blue eyes would sometimes be raised as if to pierce the depths of that gloomy staircase and those damp store-rooms. After sounding the profound cloistral silence, she seemed to be listening to remote, inarticulate revelations of the life of passion, which accounts feelings as of higher value than things. And at such moments her cheek would flush, her idle hands would lay the muslin sewing on the polished oak counter, and presently her mother would say in a voice, of which even the softest tones were sour, "Augustine, my treasure, what are you thinking about?" It is possible that two romances discovered by Augustine in the cupboard of a cook Madame Guillaume had lately discharged—Hippolyte Comte de Douglas and Le Comte de Comminges—may have contributed to develop the ideas of the young girl, who had devoured them in secret, during the long nights of the past winter.

And so Augustine's expression of vague longing, her gentle voice, her jasmine skin, and her blue eyes had lighted in poor Lebas' soul a flame as ardent as it was reverent. From an easily understood caprice, Augustine felt no affection for the orphan; perhaps she did not know that he loved her. On the other hand, the senior apprentice, with his long legs, his chestnut hair, his big hands and powerful frame, had found a secret admirer in Mademoiselle Virginie, who, in spite of her dower of fifty thousand crowns, had as yet no suitor. Nothing could be more natural than these two passions at cross-purposes, born in the silence of the dingy shop, as violets bloom in the depths of a wood. The mute and constant looks which made the young people's eyes meet by sheer need of change in the midst of persistent work and cloistered peace, was sure, sooner or later, to give rise to feelings of love. The habit of seeing always the same face leads insensibly to our reading there the qualities of the soul, and at last effaces all its defects.

"At the pace at which that man goes, our girls will soon have to go on their knees to a suitor!" said Monsieur Guillaume to himself, as he read the first decree by which Napoleon drew in advance on the conscript classes.

From that day the old merchant, grieved at seeing his eldest daughter fade, remembered how he had married Mademoiselle Chevrel under much the same circumstances as those of Joseph Lebas and Virginie. A good bit of business, to marry off his daughter, and discharge a sacred debt by repaying to an orphan the benefit he had formerly received from his predecessor under similar conditions! Joseph Lebas, who was now three-and-thirty, was aware of the obstacle which a difference of fifteen years placed between Augustine and himself. Being also too clear-sighted not to understand Monsieur Guillaume's purpose, he knew his inexorable principles well enough to feel sure that the second would never marry before the elder. So the hapless assistant, whose heart was as warm as his legs were long and his chest deep, suffered in silence.

This was the state of the affairs in the tiny republic which, in the heart of the Rue Saint-Denis, was not unlike a dependency of La Trappe. But to give a full account of events as well as of feelings, it is needful to go back to some months before the scene with which this story opens. At dusk one evening, a young man passing the darkened shop of the Cat and Racket, had paused for a moment to gaze at a picture which might have arrested every painter in the world. The shop was not yet lighted, and was as a dark cave beyond which the dining-room was visible. A hanging lamp shed the yellow light which lends such charm to pictures of the Dutch school. The white linen, the silver, the cut glass, were brilliant accessories, and made more picturesque by strong contrasts of light and shade. The figures of the head of the family and his wife, the faces of the apprentices, and the pure form of Augustine, near whom a fat chubby-cheeked maid was standing, composed so strange a group; the heads were so singular, and every face had so candid an expression; it was so easy to read the peace, the silence, the modest way of life in this family, that to an artist accustomed to render nature, there was something hopeless in any attempt to depict this scene, come upon by chance. The stranger was a young painter, who, seven years before, had gained the first prize for painting. He had now just come back from Rome. His soul, full-fed with poetry; his eyes, satiated with Raphael and Michael Angelo, thirsted for real nature after long dwelling in the pompous land where art has everywhere left something grandiose. Right or wrong, this was his personal feeling. His heart, which had long been a prey to the fire of Italian passion, craved one of those modest and meditative maidens whom in Rome he had unfortunately seen only in painting. From the enthusiasm produced in his excited fancy by the living picture before him, he naturally passed to a profound admiration for the principal figure; Augustine seemed to be pensive, and did not eat; by the arrangement of the lamp the light fell full on her face, and her bust seemed to move in a circle of fire, which threw up the shape of her head and illuminated it with almost supernatural effect. The artist involuntarily compared her to an exiled angel dreaming of heaven. An almost unknown emotion, a limpid, seething love flooded his heart. After remaining a minute, overwhelmed by the weight of his ideas, he tore himself from his bliss, went home, ate nothing, and could not sleep.

The next day he went to his studio, and did not come out of it till he had placed on canvas the magic of the scene of which the memory had, in a sense, made him a devotee; his happiness was incomplete till he should possess a faithful portrait of his idol. He went many times past the house of the Cat and Racket; he even ventured in once or twice, under a disguise, to get a closer view of the bewitching creature that Madame Guillaume covered with her wing. For eight whole months, devoted to his love and to his brush, he was lost to the sight of his most intimate friends forgetting the world, the theatre, poetry, music, and all his dearest habits. One morning Girodet broke through all the barriers with which artists are familiar, and which they know how to evade, went into his room, and woke him by asking, "What are you going to send to the Salon?" The artist grasped his friend's hand, dragged him off to the studio, uncovered a small easel picture and a portrait. After a long and eager study of the two masterpieces, Girodet threw himself on his comrade's neck and hugged him, without speaking a word. His feelings could only be expressed as he felt them—soul to soul.

"You are in love?" said Girodet.

They both knew that the finest portraits by Titian, Raphael, and Leonardo da Vinci, were the outcome of the enthusiastic sentiments by which, indeed, under various conditions, every masterpiece is engendered. The artist only bent his head in reply.

"How happy are you to be able to be in love, here, after coming back from Italy! But I do not advise you to send such works as these to the Salon," the great painter went on. "You see, these two works will not be appreciated. Such true coloring, such prodigious work, cannot yet be understood; the public is not accustomed to such depths. The pictures we paint, my dear fellow, are mere screens. We should do better to turn rhymes, and translate the antique poets! There is more glory to be looked for there than from our luckless canvases!"

Notwithstanding this charitable advice, the two pictures were exhibited. The Interior made a revolution in painting. It gave birth to the pictures of genre which pour into all our exhibitions in such prodigious quantity that they might be supposed to be produced by machinery. As to the portrait, few artists have forgotten that lifelike work; and the public, which as a body is sometimes discerning, awarded it the crown which Girodet himself had hung over it. The two pictures were surrounded by a vast throng. They fought for places, as women say. Speculators and moneyed men would have covered the canvas with double napoleons, but the artist obstinately refused to sell or to make replicas. An enormous sum was offered him for the right of engraving them, and the print-sellers were not more favored than the amateurs.

Though these incidents occupied the world, they were not of a nature to penetrate the recesses of the monastic solitude in the Rue Saint-Denis. However, when paying a visit to Madame Guillaume, the notary's wife spoke of the exhibition before Augustine, of whom she was very fond, and explained its purpose. Madame Roguin's gossip naturally inspired Augustine with a wish to see the pictures, and with courage enough to ask her cousin secretly to take her to the Louvre. Her cousin succeeded in the negotiations she opened with Madame Guillaume for permission to release the young girl for two hours from her dull labors. Augustine was thus able to make her way through the crowd to see the crowned work. A fit of trembling shook her like an aspen leaf as she recognized herself. She was terrified, and looked about her to find Madame Roguin, from whom she had been separated by a tide of people. At that moment her frightened eyes fell on the impassioned face of the young painter. She at once recalled the figure of a loiterer whom, being curious, she had frequently observed, believing him to be a new neighbor.

"You see how love has inspired me," said the artist in the timid creature's ear, and she stood in dismay at the words.

She found supernatural courage to enable her to push through the crowd and join her cousin, who was still struggling with the mass of people that hindered her from getting to the picture.

"You will be stifled!" cried Augustine. "Let us go."

But there are moments, at the Salon, when two women

are not always free to direct their steps through the galleries. By the irregular course to which they were compelled by the press, Mademoiselle Guillaume and her cousin were pushed to within a few steps of the second picture. Chance thus brought them, both together, to where they could easily see the canvas made famous by fashion, for once in agreement with talent. Madame Roguin's exclamation of surprise was lost in the hubbub and buzz of the crowd; Augustine involuntarily shed tears at the sight of this wonderful study. Then, by an almost unaccountable impulse, she laid her finger on her lips, as she perceived quite near her the ecstatic face of the young painter. The stranger replied by a nod, and pointed to Madame Roguin, as a spoil-sport, to show Augustine that he had understood. This pantomime struck the young girl like hot coals on her flesh; she felt quite guilty as she perceived that there was a compact between herself and the artist. The suffocating heat, the dazzling sight of beautiful dresses, the bewilderment produced in Augustine's brain by the truth of coloring, the multitude of living or painted figures, the profusion of gilt frames, gave her a sense of intoxication which doubled her alarms. She would perhaps have fainted if an unknown rapture had not surged up in her heart to vivify her whole being, in spite of this chaos of sensations. She nevertheless believed herself to be under the power of the Devil, of whose awful snares she had been warned of by the thundering words of preachers. This moment was to her like a moment of madness. She found herself accompanied to her cousin's carriage by the young man, radiant with joy and love. Augustine, a prey to an agitation new to her experience, an intoxication which seemed to abandon her to nature, listened to the eloquent voice of her heart, and looked again and again at the young painter, betraying the emotion that came over her. Never had the bright rose of her cheeks shown in stronger contrast with the whiteness of her skin. The artist saw her beauty in all its bloom, her maiden modesty in all its glory. She herself felt a sort of rapture mingled with terror at thinking that her presence had brought happiness to him whose name was on every lip, and whose talent lent immortality to transient scenes. She was loved! It was impossible to doubt it. When she no longer saw the artist, these simple words still echoed in her ear, "You see how love has inspired me!" And the throbs of her heart, as they grew deeper, seemed a pain, her heated blood revealed so many unknown forces in her being. She affected a severe headache to avoid replying to her cousin's questions concerning the pictures; but on their return Madame Roguin could not forbear from speaking to Madame Guillaume of the fame that had fallen on the house of the Cat and Racket, and Augustine quaked in every limb as she heard her mother say that she should go to the Salon to see her house there. The young girl again declared herself suffering, and obtained leave to go to bed.

"That is what comes of sight-seeing," exclaimed Monsieur Guillaume—"a headache. And is it so very amusing to see in a picture what you can see any day in your own street? Don't talk to me of your artists! Like writers, they are a starveling crew. Why the devil need they choose my house to flout it in their pictures?"

"It may help to sell a few ells more of cloth," said Joseph Lebas.

This remark did not protect art and thought from being condemned once again before the judgment-seat of trade. As may be supposed, these speeches did not infuse much hope into Augustine, who, during the night, gave herself up to the first meditations of love. The events of the day were like a dream, which it was a joy to recall to her mind. She was initiated into the fears, the hopes, the remorse, all the ebb and flow of feeling which could not fail to toss a heart so simple and timid as hers. What a void she perceived in this gloomy house!

What a treasure she found in her soul! To be the wife of a genius, to share his glory! What ravages must such a vision make in the heart of a girl brought up among such a family! What hopes must it raise in a young creature who, in the midst of sordid elements, had pined for a life of elegance! A sunbeam had fallen into the prison. Augustine was suddenly in love. So many of her feelings were soothed that she succumbed without reflection. At eighteen does not love hold a prism between the world and the eyes of a young girl? She was incapable of suspecting the hard facts which result from the union of a loving woman with a man of imagination, and she believed herself called to make him happy, not seeing any disparity between herself and him. To her the future would be as the present. When, next day, her father and mother returned from the Salon, their dejected faces proclaimed some disappointment. In the first place, the painter had removed the two pictures; and then Madame Guillaume had lost her cashmere shawl. But the news that the pictures had disappeared from the walls since her visit revealed to Augustine a delicacy of sentiment which a woman can always appreciate, even by instinct.

On the morning when, on his way home from a ball, Theodore de Sommervieux—for this was the name which fame had stamped on Augustine's heart—had been squirted on by the apprentices while awaiting the appearance of his artless little friend, who certainly did not know that he was there, the lovers had seen each other for the fourth time only since their meeting at the Salon. The difficulties which the rule of the house placed in the way of the painter's ardent nature gave added violence to his passion for Augustine.

How could he get near to a young girl seated in a counting-house between two such women as Mademoiselle Virginie and Madame Guillaume? How could he correspond with her when her mother never left her side? Ingenious, as lovers are, to imagine woes, Theodore saw a rival in one of the assistants, to whose interests he supposed the others to be devoted. If he should evade these sons of Argus, he would yet be wrecked under the stern eye of the old draper or of Madame Guillaume. The very vehemence of his passion hindered the young painter from hitting on the ingenious expedients which, in prisoners and in lovers, seem to be the last effort of intelligence spurred by a wild craving for liberty, or by the fire of love. Theodore wandered about the neighborhood with the restlessness of a madman, as though movement might inspire him with some device. After racking his imagination, it occurred to him to bribe the blowsy waiting-maid with gold. Thus a few notes were exchanged at long intervals during the fortnight following the ill-starred morning when Monsieur Guillaume and Theodore had so scrutinized one another. At the present moment the young couple had agreed to see each other at a certain hour of the day, and on Sunday, at Saint-Leu, during Mass and vespers. Augustine had sent her dear Theodore a list of the relations and friends of the family, to whom the young painter tried to get access, in the hope of interesting, if it were possible, in his love affairs, one of these souls absorbed in money and trade, to whom a genuine passion must appear a quite monstrous speculation, a thing unheard-of. Nothing meanwhile, was altered at the sign of the Cat and Racket. If Augustine was absent-minded, if, against all obedience to the domestic code, she stole up to her room to make signals by means of a jar of flowers, if she sighed, if she were lost in thought, no one observed it, not even her mother. This will cause some surprise to those who have entered into the spirit of the household, where an idea tainted with poetry would be in startling contrast to persons and things, where no one could venture on a gesture or a look which would not be seen and analyzed. Nothing, however, could be more natural: the quiet barque that navigated the stormy waters of the Paris Exchange, under the flag of the Cat and Racket, was just now in the toils of one of these tempests which, returning periodically, might be termed equinoctial. For the last fortnight the five men forming the crew, with Madame Guillaume and Mademoiselle Virginie, had been devoting themselves to the hard labor, known as stock-taking.

Every bale was turned over, and the length verified to ascertain the exact value of the remnant. The ticket attached to each parcel was carefully examined to see at what time the piece had been bought. The retail price was fixed. Monsieur Guillaume, always on his feet, his pen behind his ear, was like a captain commanding the working of the ship. His sharp tones, spoken through a trap-door, to inquire into the depths of the hold in the cellar-store, gave utterance to the barbarous formulas of trade-jargon, which find expression only in cipher. "How much H. N. Z.?"—"All sold."—"What is left of Q. X.?"—"Two ells."—"At what price?"—"Fifty-five three."— "Set down A. at three, with all of J. J., all of M. P., and what is left of V. D. O."—A hundred other injunctions equally intelligible were spouted over the counters like verses of modern poetry, quoted by romantic spirits, to excite each other's enthusiasm for one of their poets. In the evening Guillaume, shut up with his assistant and his wife, balanced his accounts, carried on the balance, wrote to debtors in arrears, and made out bills. All three were busy over this enormous labor, of which the result could be stated on a sheet of foolscap, proving to the head of the house that there was so much to the good in hard cash, so much in goods, so much in bills and notes; that he did not owe a sou; that a hundred or two hundred thousand francs were owing to him; that the capital had been increased; that the farmlands, the houses, or the investments were extended, or repaired, or doubled. Whence it became necessary to begin again with increased ardor, to accumulate more crown-pieces, without its ever entering the brain of these laborious ants to ask—"To what end?"

Favored by this annual turmoil, the happy Augustine escaped the investigations of her Argus-eyed relations. At last, one Saturday evening, the stock-taking was finished. The figures of the sum-total showed a row of 0"s long enough to allow Guillaume for once to relax the stern rule as to dessert which reigned throughout the year. The shrewd old draper rubbed his hands, and allowed his assistants to remain at table. The members of the crew had hardly swallowed their thimbleful of some home-made liqueur, when the rumble of a carriage was heard. The family party were going to see Cendrillon at the Varietes, while the two younger apprentices each received a crown of six francs, with permission to go wherever they chose, provided they were in by midnight.

Notwithstanding this debauch, the old cloth-merchant was shaving himself at six next morning, put on his maroon-colored coat, of which the glowing lights afforded him perennial enjoyment, fastened a pair of gold buckles on the knee-straps of his ample satin breeches; and then, at about seven o'clock, while all were still sleeping in the house, he made his way to the little office adjoining the shop on the first floor. Daylight came in through a window, fortified by iron bars, and looking out on a small yard surrounded by such black walls that it was very like a well. The old merchant opened the iron-lined shutters, which were so familiar to him, and threw up the lower half of the sash window. The icy air of the courtyard came in to cool the hot atmosphere of the little room, full of the odor peculiar to offices.

The merchant remained standing, his hand resting on the greasy arm of a large cane chair lined with morocco, of which the original hue had disappeared; he seemed to hesitate as to seating himself. He looked with affection at the double desk, where his wife's seat, opposite his own, was fitted into a little niche in the wall. He

contemplated the numbered boxes, the files, the imple-
ments, the cash box—objects all of immemorial origin,
and fancied himself in the room with the shade of Master
Chevrel. He even pulled out the high stool on which he
had once sat in the presence of his departed master.
This stool, covered with black leather, the horse-hair
showing at every corner—as it had long done, without,
however, coming out—he placed with a shaking hand
on the very spot where his predecessor had put it, and
then, with an emotion difficult to describe, he pulled a
bell, which rang at the head of Joseph Lebas' bed. When
this decisive blow had been struck, the old man, for
whom, no doubt, these reminiscences were too much,
took up three or four bills of exchange, and looked at
them without seeing them.

Suddenly Joseph Lebas stood before him.

"Sit down there," said Guillaume, pointing to the stool.

As the old master draper had never yet bid his assistant
be seated in his presence, Joseph Lebas was startled.

"What do you think of these notes?" asked Guillaume.

"They will never be paid."

"Why?"

"Well, I heard the day before yesterday Etienne and
Co. had made their payments in gold."

"Oh, oh!" said the draper. "Well, one must be very ill
to show one's bile. Let us speak of something else.—
Joseph, the stock-taking is done."

"Yes, monsieur, and the dividend is one of the best
you have ever made."

"Do not use new-fangled words. Say the profits,
Joseph. Do you know, my boy, that this result is partly
owing to you? And I do not intend to pay you a salary
any longer. Madame Guillaume has suggested to me to

take you into partnership.—'Guillaume and Lebas;' will not that make a good business name? We might add, 'and Co.' to round off the firm's signature."

Tears rose to the eyes of Joseph Lebas, who tried to hide them.

"Oh, Monsieur Guillaume, how have I deserved such kindness? I only do my duty. It was so much already that you should take an interest in a poor orph——"

He was brushing the cuff of his left sleeve with his right hand, and dared not look at the old man, who smiled as he thought that this modest young fellow no doubt needed, as he had needed once on a time, some encouragement to complete his explanation.

"To be sure," said Virginie's father, "you do not altogether deserve this favor, Joseph. You have not so much confidence in me as I have in you." (The young man looked up quickly.) "You know all the secrets of the cash-box. For the last two years I have told you almost all my concerns. I have sent you to travel in our goods. In short, I have nothing on my conscience as regards you. But you—you have a soft place, and you have never breathed a word of it." Joseph Lebas blushed. "Ah, ha!" cried Guillaume, "so you thought you could deceive an old fox like me? When you knew that I had scented the Lecocq bankruptcy?"

"What, monsieur?" replied Joseph Lebas, looking at his master as keenly as his master looked at him, "you knew that I was in love?"

"I know everything, you rascal," said the worthy and cunning old merchant, pulling the assistant's ear. "And I forgive you—I did the same myself."

"And you will give her to me?"

"Yes—with fifty thousand crowns; and I will leave you as much by will, and we will start on our new career under the name of a new firm. We will do good business yet, my boy!" added the old man, getting up and flourishing his arms. "I tell you, son-in-law, there is nothing like trade. Those who ask what pleasure is to be found in it are simpletons. To be on the scent of a good bargain, to hold your own on 'Change, to watch as anxiously as at the gaming-table whether Etienne and Co. will fail or no, to see a regiment of Guards march past all dressed in your cloth, to trip your neighbor up—honestly of course!—to make the goods cheaper than others can; then to carry out an undertaking which you have planned, which begins, grows, totters, and succeeds! to know the workings of every house of business as well as a minister of police, so as never to make a mistake; to hold up your head in the midst of wrecks, to have friends by correspondence in every manufacturing town; is not that a perpetual game, Joseph? That is life, that is! I shall die in that harness, like old Chevrel, but taking it easy now, all the same."

In the heat of his eager rhetoric, old Guillaume had scarcely looked at his assistant, who was weeping copiously. "Why, Joseph, my poor boy, what is the matter?"

"Oh, I love her so! Monsieur Guillaume, that my heart fails me; I believe——"

"Well, well, boy," said the old man, touched, "you are happier than you know, by God! For she loves you. I know it."

And he blinked his little green eyes as he looked at the young man.

"Mademoiselle Augustine! Mademoiselle Augustine!" exclaimed Joseph Lebas in his rapture.

He was about to rush out of the room when he felt himself clutched by a hand of iron, and his astonished master spun him round in front of him once more.

"What has Augustine to do with this matter?" he asked, in a voice which instantly froze the luckless Joseph.

"Is it not she that—that—I love?" stammered the assistant.

Much put out by his own want of perspicacity, Guillaume sat down again, and rested his long head in his hands to consider the perplexing situation in which he found himself. Joseph Lebas, shamefaced and in despair, remained standing.

"Joseph," the draper said with frigid dignity, "I was speaking of Virginie. Love cannot be made to order, I know. I know, too, that you can be trusted. We will forget all this. I will not let Augustine marry before Virginie.—Your interest will be ten per cent."

The young man, to whom love gave I know not what power of courage and eloquence, clasped his hand, and spoke in his turn—spoke for a quarter of an hour, with so much warmth and feeling, that he altered the situation. If the question had been a matter of business the old tradesman would have had fixed principles to guide his decision; but, tossed a thousand miles from commerce, on the ocean of sentiment, without a compass, he floated, as he told himself, undecided in the face of such an unexpected event. Carried away by his fatherly kindness, he began to beat about the bush.

"Deuce take it, Joseph, you must know that there are ten years between my two children. Mademoiselle Chevrel was no beauty, still she has had nothing to complain of in me. Do as I did. Come, come, don't cry. Can you be so silly? What is to be done? It can be managed perhaps. There is always some way out of a scrape. And we men are not always devoted Celadons to our wives—you understand? Madame Guillaume is very pious. ... Come. By Gad, boy, give your arm to Augustine this morning as we go to Mass."

These were the phrases spoken at random by the old draper, and their conclusion made the lover happy. He was already thinking of a friend of his as a match for Mademoiselle Virginie, as he went out of the smoky office, pressing his future father-in-law's hand, after saying with a knowing look that all would turn out for the best.

"What will Madame Guillaume say to it?" was the idea that greatly troubled the worthy merchant when he found himself alone.

At breakfast Madame Guillaume and Virginie, to whom the draper had not yet confided his disappointment, cast meaning glances at Joseph Lebas, who was extremely embarrassed. The young assistant's bashfulness commended him to his mother-in-law's good graces. The matron became so cheerful that she smiled as she looked at her husband, and allowed herself some little pleasantries of time-honored acceptance in such simple families. She wondered whether Joseph or Virginie were the taller, to ask them to compare their height. This preliminary fooling brought a cloud to the master's brow, and he even made such a point of decorum that he desired Augustine to take the assistant's arm on their way to Saint-Leu. Madame Guillaume, surprised at this manly delicacy, honored her husband with a nod of approval. So the procession left the house in such order as to suggest no suspicious meaning to the neighbors.

"Does it not seem to you, Mademoiselle Augustine," said the assistant, and he trembled, "that the wife of a merchant whose credit is as good as Monsieur Guillaume's, for instance, might enjoy herself a little more than Madame your mother does? Might wear diamonds— or keep a carriage? For my part, if I were to marry, I should be glad to take all the work, and see my wife happy. I would not put her into the counting-house. In the drapery business, you see, a woman is not so necessary now as formerly. Monsieur Guillaume was quite right to act as he did—and besides, his wife liked it. But so long as a woman knows how to turn her hand to the book-keeping, the correspondence, the retail business, the orders, and her housekeeping, so as not to sit idle, that is enough. At seven o'clock, when the shop is shut, I shall take my pleasures, go to the play, and into company.—But you are not listening to me."

"Yes, indeed, Monsieur Joseph. What do you think of painting? That is a fine calling."

"Yes. I know a master house-painter, Monsieur Lourdois. He is well-to-do."

Thus conversing, the family reached the Church of Saint-Leu. There Madame Guillaume reasserted her rights, and, for the first time, placed Augustine next herself, Virginie taking her place on the fourth chair, next to Lebas. During the sermon all went well between Augustine and Theodore, who, standing behind a pillar, worshiped his Madonna with fervent devotion; but at the elevation of the Host, Madame Guillaume discovered, rather late, that her daughter Augustine was holding her prayer-book upside down. She was about to speak to her strongly, when, lowering her veil, she interrupted her own devotions to look in the direction where her daughter's eyes found attraction. By the help of her spectacles she saw the young artist, whose fashionable elegance seemed to proclaim him a cavalry officer on leave rather than a tradesman of the neighborhood. It is difficult to conceive of the state of violent agitation in which Madame Guillaume found herself—she, who flattered herself on having brought up her daughters to perfection—on discovering in Augustine a clandestine passion of which her prudery and ignorance exaggerated the perils. She believed her daughter to be cankered to the core.

"Hold your book right way up, miss," she muttered in a low voice, tremulous with wrath. She snatched away

the tell-tale prayer-book and returned it with the let-
ter-press right way up. "Do not allow your eyes to look
anywhere but at your prayers," she added, "or I shall
have something to say to you. Your father and I will talk
to you after church."

These words came like a thunderbolt on poor Augustine. She felt faint; but, torn between the distress she felt
and the dread of causing a commotion in church she
bravely concealed her anguish. It was, however, easy to
discern the stormy state of her soul from the trembling
of her prayer-book, and the tears which dropped on
every page she turned. From the furious glare shot at
him by Madame Guillaume the artist saw the peril into
which his love affair had fallen; he went out, with a
raging soul, determined to venture all.

"Go to your room, miss!" said Madame Guillaume, on
their return home; "we will send for you, but take care
not to quit it."

The conference between the husband and wife was
conducted so secretly that at first nothing was heard of
it. Virginie, however, who had tried to give her sister
courage by a variety of gentle remonstrances, carried
her good nature so far as to listen at the door of her
mother's bedroom where the discussion was held, to
catch a word or two. The first time she went down to
the lower floor she heard her father exclaim, "Then,
madame, do you wish to kill your daughter?"

"My poor dear!" said Virginie, in tears, "papa takes
your part."

"And what do they want to do to Theodore?" asked
the innocent girl.

Virginie, inquisitive, went down again; but this time
she stayed longer; she learned that Joseph Lebas loved
Augustine. It was written that on this memorable day,
this house, generally so peaceful, should be a hell. Mon-

sieur Guillaume brought Joseph Lebas to despair by tell-
ing him of Augustine's love for a stranger. Lebas, who
had advised his friend to become a suitor for Mademoiselle Virginie, saw all his hopes wrecked. Mademoiselle Virginie, overcome by hearing that Joseph had, in
a way, refused her, had a sick headache. The dispute
that had arisen from the discussion between Monsieur
and Madame Guillaume, when, for the third time in
their lives, they had been of antagonistic opinions, had
shown itself in a terrible form. Finally, at half-past four
in the afternoon, Augustine, pale, trembling, and with
red eyes, was haled before her father and mother. The
poor child artlessly related the too brief tale of her love.
Reassured by a speech from her father, who promised
to listen to her in silence, she gathered courage as she
pronounced to her parents the name of Theodore de
Sommervieux, with a mischievous little emphasis on the
aristocratic de. And yielding to the unknown charm of
talking of her feelings, she was brave enough to declare
with innocent decision that she loved Monsieur de Sommervieux, that she had written to him, and she added,
with tears in her eyes: "To sacrifice me to another man
would make me wretched."

"But, Augustine, you cannot surely know what a
painter is?" cried her mother with horror.

"Madame Guillaume!" said the old man, compelling
her to silence.—"Augustine," he went on, "artists are
generally little better than beggars. They are too extrav-
agant not to be always a bad sort. I served the late Monsieur Joseph Vernet, the late Monsieur Lekain, and the
late Monsieur Noverre. Oh, if you could only know the
tricks played on poor Father Chevrel by that Monsieur
Noverre, by the Chevalier de Saint-Georges, and especially by Monsieur Philidor! They are a set of rascals; I
know them well! They all have a gab and nice manners.
Ah, your Monsieur Sumer—, Somm——"

"De Sommervieux, papa."

"Well, well, de Sommervieux, well and good. He can never have been half so sweet to you as Monsieur le Chevalier de Saint-Georges was to me the day I got a verdict of the consuls against him. And in those days they were gentlemen of quality."

"But, father, Monsieur Theodore is of good family, and he wrote me that he is rich; his father was called Chevalier de Sommervieux before the Revolution."

At these words Monsieur Guillaume looked at his terrible better half, who, like an angry woman, sat tapping the floor with her foot while keeping sullen silence; she avoided even casting wrathful looks at Augustine, appearing to leave to Monsieur Guillaume the whole responsibility in so grave a matter, since her opinion was not listened to. Nevertheless, in spite of her apparent self-control, when she saw her husband giving way so mildly under a catastrophe which had no concern with business, she exclaimed:

"Really, monsieur, you are so weak with your daughters! However——"

The sound of a carriage, which stopped at the door, interrupted the rating which the old draper already quaked at. In a minute Madame Roguin was standing in the middle of the room, and looking at the actors in this domestic scene: "I know all, my dear cousin," said she, with a patronizing air.

Madame Roguin made the great mistake of supposing that a Paris notary's wife could play the part of a favorite of fashion.

"I know all," she repeated, "and I have come into Noah's Ark, like the dove, with the olive-branch. I read that allegory in the Genie du Christianisme," she added, turning to Madame Guillaume; "the allusion ought to please you, cousin. Do you know," she went on, smiling at Augustine, "that Monsieur de Sommervieux is a charming man? He gave me my portrait this morning, painted by a master's hand. It is worth at least six thousand francs." And at these words she patted Monsieur Guillaume on the arm. The old draper could not help making a grimace with his lips, which was peculiar to him.

"I know Monsieur de Sommervieux very well," the Dove ran on. "He has come to my evenings this fortnight past, and made them delightful. He has told me all his woes, and commissioned me to plead for him. I know since this morning that he adores Augustine, and he shall have her. Ah, cousin, do not shake your head in refusal. He will be created Baron, I can tell you, and has just been made Chevalier of the Legion of Honor, by the Emperor himself, at the Salon. Roguin is now his lawyer, and knows all his affairs. Well! Monsieur de Sommervieux has twelve thousand francs a year in good landed estate. Do you know that the father-in-law of such a man may get a rise in life—be mayor of his arrondissement, for instance. Have we not seen Monsieur Dupont become a Count of the Empire, and a senator, all because he went as mayor to congratulate the Emperor on his entry into Vienna? Oh, this marriage must take place! For my part, I adore the dear young man. His behavior to Augustine is only met with in romances. Be easy, little one, you shall be happy, and every girl will wish she were in your place. Madame la Duchesse de Carigliano, who comes to my 'At Homes,' raves about Monsieur de Sommervieux. Some spiteful people say she only comes to me to meet him; as if a duchess of yesterday was doing too much honor to a Chevrel, whose family have been respected citizens these hundred years!

"Augustine," Madame Roguin went on, after a short pause, "I have seen the portrait. Heavens! How lovely it is! Do you know that the Emperor wanted to have it? He laughed, and said to the Deputy High Constable that if there were many women like that in his court while all the kings visited it, he should have no difficulty about preserving the peace of Europe. Is not that a compliment?"

The tempests with which the day had begun were to resemble those of nature, by ending in clear and serene weather. Madame Roguin displayed so much address in her harangue, she was able to touch so many strings in the dry hearts of Monsieur and Madame Guillaume, that at last she hit on one which she could work upon. At this strange period commerce and finance were more than ever possessed by the crazy mania for seeking alliance with rank; and the generals of the Empire took full advantage of this desire. Monsieur Guillaume, as a singular exception, opposed this deplorable craving. His favorite axioms were that, to secure happiness, a woman must marry a man of her own class; that every one was punished sooner or later for having climbed too high; that love could so little endure under the worries of a household, that both husband and wife needed sound good qualities to be happy, that it would not do for one to be far in advance of the other, because, above everything, they must understand each other; if a man spoke Greek and his wife Latin, they might come to die of hunger. He had himself invented this sort of adage. And he compared such marriages to old-fashioned materials of mixed silk and wool. Still, there is so much vanity at the bottom of man's heart that the prudence of the pilot who steered the Cat and Racket so wisely gave way before Madame Roguin's aggressive volubility. Austere Madame Guillaume was the first to see in her daughter's affection a reason for abdicating her principles and for consenting to receive Monsieur de Sommervieux, whom she promised herself she would put under severe inquisition.

The old draper went to look for Joseph Lebas, and inform him of the state of affairs. At half-past six, the dining-room immortalized by the artist saw, united under its skylight, Monsieur and Madame Roguin, the young painter and his charming Augustine, Joseph Lebas, who found his happiness in patience, and Mademoiselle Virginie, convalescent from her headache. Monsieur and Madame Guillaume saw in perspective both their children married, and the fortunes of the Cat and Racket once more in skilful hands. Their satisfaction was at its height when, at dessert, Theodore made them a present of the wonderful picture which they had failed to see, representing the interior of the old shop, and to which they all owed so much happiness.

"Isn't it pretty!" cried Guillaume. "And to think that any one would pay thirty thousand francs for that!"

"Because you can see my lappets in it," said Madame Guillaume.

"And the cloth unrolled!" added Lebas; "you might take it up in your hand."

"Drapery always comes out well," replied the painter. "We should be only too happy, we modern artists, if we could touch the perfection of antique drapery."

"So you like drapery!" cried old Guillaume. "Well, then, by Gad! shake hands on that, my young friend. Since you can respect trade, we shall understand each other. And why should it be despised? The world began with trade, since Adam sold Paradise for an apple. He did not strike a good bargain though!" And the old man roared with honest laughter, encouraged by the champagne, which he sent round with a liberal hand. The band that covered the young artist's eyes was so thick that he thought his future parents amiable. He was not above enlivening them by a few jests in the best taste. So he too pleased every one. In the evening, when the drawing-room, furnished with what Madame Guillaume called "everything handsome," was deserted, and while she flitted from the table to the chimney-piece, from the candelabra to the tall candlesticks, hastily blowing out the wax-lights, the worthy draper, who was always clear-sighted when money was in question, called Augustine to him, and seating her on his knee, spoke as follows:—

"My dear child, you shall marry your Sommervieux since you insist; you may, if you like, risk your capital in happiness. But I am not going to be hoodwinked by the thirty thousand francs to be made by spoiling good canvas. Money that is lightly earned is lightly spent. Did I not hear that hare-brained youngster declare this evening that money was made round that it might roll. If it is round for spendthrifts, it is flat for saving folks who pile it up. Now, my child, that fine gentleman talks of giving you carriages and diamonds! He has money, let him spend it on you; so be it. It is no concern of mine. But as to what I can give you, I will not have the crown-pieces I have picked up with so much toil wasted in carriages and frippery. Those who spend too fast never grow rich. A hundred thousand crowns, which is your fortune, will not buy up Paris. It is all very well to look forward to a few hundred thousand francs to be yours some day; I shall keep you waiting for them as long as possible, by Gad! So I took your lover aside, and a man who managed the Lecocq bankruptcy had not much difficulty in persuading the artist to marry under a settlement of his wife's money on herself. I will keep an eye on the marriage contract to see that what he is to settle on you is safely tied up. So now, my child, I hope to be a grandfather, by Gad! I will begin at once to lay up for my grandchildren; but swear to me, here and now, never to sign any papers relating to money without my advice; and if I go soon to join old Father Chevrel, promise to consult young Lebas, your brother-in-law."

"Yes, father, I swear it."

At these words, spoken in a gentle voice, the old man kissed his daughter on both cheeks. That night the lovers slept as soundly as Monsieur and Madame Guillaume.

Some few months after this memorable Sunday the high altar of Saint-Leu was the scene of two very different weddings. Augustine and Theodore appeared in all the radiance of happiness, their eyes beaming with love, dressed with elegance, while a fine carriage waited for them. Virginie, who had come in a good hired fly with the rest of the family, humbly followed her younger sister, dressed in the simplest fashion like a shadow necessary to the harmony of the picture. Monsieur Guillaume had exerted himself to the utmost in the church to get Virginie married before Augustine, but the priests, high and low, persisted in addressing the more elegant of the two brides. He heard some of his neighbors highly approving the good sense of Mademoiselle Virginie, who was making, as they said, the more substantial match, and remaining faithful to the neighborhood; while they fired a few taunts, prompted by envy of Augustine, who was marrying an artist and a man of rank; adding, with a sort of dismay, that if the Guillaumes were ambitious, there was an end to the business. An old fan-maker having remarked that such a prodigal would soon bring his wife to beggary, father Guillaume prided himself in petto for his prudence in the matter of marriage settlements. In the evening, after a splendid ball, followed by one of those substantial suppers of which the memory is dying out in the present generation, Monsieur and Madame Guillaume remained in a fine house belonging to them in the Rue du Colombier, where the wedding had been held; Monsieur and Madame Lebas returned in their fly to the old home in the Rue Saint-Denis, to steer the good ship Cat and Racket. The artist, intoxicated with happiness, carried off his beloved Augustine, and eagerly lifting her out of their carriage when it reached the Rue des Trois-Freres, led her to an apartment embellished by all the arts.

The fever of passion which possessed Theodore made a year fly over the young couple without a single cloud to dim the blue sky under which they lived. Life did not hang heavy on the lovers' hands. Theodore lavished on every day inexhaustible fioriture of enjoyment, and he delighted to vary the transports of passion by the soft languor of those hours of repose when souls soar so high that they seem to have forgotten all bodily union. Augustine was too happy for reflection; she floated on an undulating tide of rapture; she thought she could not do enough by abandoning herself to sanctioned and sacred married love; simple and artless, she had no coquetry, no reserves, none of the dominion which a worldly-minded girl acquires over her husband by ingenious caprice; she loved too well to calculate for the future, and never imagined that so exquisite a life could come to an end. Happy in being her husband's sole delight, she believed that her inextinguishable love would always be her greatest grace in his eyes, as her devotion and obedience would be a perennial charm. And, indeed, the ecstasy of love had made her so brilliantly lovely that her beauty filled her with pride, and gave her confidence that she could always reign over a man so easy to kindle as Monsieur de Sommervieux. Thus her position as a wife brought her no knowledge but the lessons of love.

In the midst of her happiness, she was still the simple child who had lived in obscurity in the Rue Saint-Denis, and who never thought of acquiring the manners, the information, the tone of the world she had to live in. Her words being the words of love, she revealed in them, no doubt, a certain pliancy of mind and a certain refinement of speech; but she used the language common to all women when they find themselves plunged in passion, which seems to be their element. When, by chance, Augustine expressed an idea that did not harmonize with Theodore's, the young artist laughed, as we laugh at the first mistakes of a foreigner, though they end by annoying us if they are not corrected.

In spite of all this love-making, by the end of this year, as delightful as it was swift, Sommervieux felt one morning the need for resuming his work and his old habits. His wife was expecting their first child. He saw some friends again. During the tedious discomforts of the year when a young wife is nursing an infant for the first time, he worked, no doubt, with zeal, but he occasionally sought diversion in the fashionable world. The house which he was best pleased to frequent was that of the Duchesse de Carigliano, who had at last attracted the celebrated artist to her parties. When Augustine was quite well again, and her boy no longer required the assiduous care which debars a mother from social pleasures, Theodore had come to the stage of wishing to know the joys of satisfied vanity to be found in society by a man who shows himself with a handsome woman, the object of envy and admiration.

To figure in drawing-rooms with the reflected lustre of her husband's fame, and to find other women envious of her, was to Augustine a new harvest of pleasures; but it was the last gleam of conjugal happiness. She first wounded her husband's vanity when, in spite of vain efforts, she betrayed her ignorance, the inelegance of her language, and the narrowness of her ideas. Sommervieux's nature, subjugated for nearly two years and a half by the first transports of love, now, in the calm of less new possession, recovered its bent and habits, for a while diverted from their channel. Poetry, painting, and the subtle joys of imagination have inalienable rights over a lofty spirit. These cravings of a powerful soul had not been starved in Theodore during these two years; they had only found fresh pasture. As soon as the meadows of love had been ransacked, and the artist had gathered roses and cornflowers as the children do, so greedily that he did not see that his hands could hold no more, the scene changed. When the painter showed his wife the sketches for his finest compositions he heard

Honoré de Balzac

her exclaim, as her father had done, "How pretty!" This tepid admiration was not the outcome of conscientious feeling, but of her faith on the strength of love.

Augustine cared more for a look than for the finest picture. The only sublime she knew was that of the heart. At last Theodore could not resist the evidence of the cruel fact—his wife was insensible to poetry, she did not dwell in his sphere, she could not follow him in all his vagaries, his inventions, his joys and his sorrows; she walked groveling in the world of reality, while his head was in the skies. Common minds cannot appreciate the perennial sufferings of a being who, while bound to another by the most intimate affections, is obliged constantly to suppress the dearest flights of his soul, and to thrust down into the void those images which a magic power compels him to create. To him the torture is all the more intolerable because his feeling towards his companion enjoins, as its first law, that they should have no concealments, but mingle the aspirations of their thought as perfectly as the effusions of their soul. The demands of nature are not to be cheated. She is as inexorable as necessity, which is, indeed, a sort of social nature. Sommervieux took refuge in the peace and silence of his studio, hoping that the habit of living with artists might mould his wife and develop in her the dormant germs of lofty intelligence which some superior minds suppose must exist in every being. But Augustine was too sincerely religious not to take fright at the tone of artists. At the first dinner Theodore gave, she heard a young painter say, with the childlike lightness, which to her was unintelligible, and which redeems a jest from the taint of profanity, "But, madame, your Paradise cannot be more beautiful than Raphael's Transfiguration!—Well, and I got tired of looking at that."

Thus Augustine came among this sparkling set in a spirit of distrust which no one could fail to see. She was a restraint on their freedom. Now an artist who feels restraint is pitiless; he stays away, or laughs it to scorn. Madame Guillaume, among other absurdities, had an excessive notion of the dignity she considered the prerogative of a married woman; and Augustine, though she had often made fun of it, could not help a slight imitation of her mother's primness. This extreme propriety, which virtuous wives do not always avoid, suggested a few epigrams in the form of sketches, in which the harmless jest was in such good taste that Sommervieux could not take offence; and even if they had been more severe, these pleasantries were after all only reprisals from his friends. Still, nothing could seem a trifle to a spirit so open as Theodore's to impressions from without. A coldness insensibly crept over him, and inevitably spread. To attain conjugal happiness we must climb a hill whose summit is a narrow ridge, close to a steep and slippery descent: the painter's love was falling down it. He regarded his wife as incapable of appreciating the moral considerations which justified him in his own eyes for his singular behavior to her, and believed himself quite innocent in hiding from her thoughts she could not enter into, and peccadilloes outside the jurisdiction of a bourgeois conscience. Augustine wrapped herself in sullen and silent grief. These unconfessed feelings placed a shroud between the husband and wife which could not fail to grow thicker day by day. Though her husband never failed in consideration for her, Augustine could not help trembling as she saw that he kept for the outer world those treasures of wit and grace that he formerly would lay at her feet. She soon began to find sinister meaning in the jocular speeches that are current in the world as to the inconstancy of men. She made no complaints, but her demeanor conveyed reproach.

Three years after her marriage this pretty young woman, who dashed past in her handsome carriage, and lived in a sphere of glory and riches to the envy of heedless folk incapable of taking a just view of the situations of life, was a prey to intense grief. She lost her color; she reflected; she made comparisons; then sorrow unfolded to her the first lessons of experience. She determined to restrict herself bravely within the round of duty, hoping that by this generous conduct she might sooner or later win back her husband's love. But it was not so. When Sommervieux, fired with work, came in from his studio, Augustine did not put away her work so quickly but that the painter might find his wife mending the household linen, and his own, with all the care of a good housewife. She supplied generously and without a murmur the money needed for his lavishness; but in her anxiety to husband her dear Theodore's fortune, she was strictly economical for herself and in certain details of domestic management. Such conduct is incompatible with the easy-going habits of artists, who, at the end of their life, have enjoyed it so keenly that they never inquire into the causes of their ruin.

It is useless to note every tint of shadow by which the brilliant hues of their honeymoon were overcast till they were lost in utter blackness. One evening poor Augustine, who had for some time heard her husband speak with enthusiasm of the Duchesse de Carigliano, received from a friend certain malignantly charitable warnings as to the nature of the attachment which Sommervieux had formed for this celebrated flirt of the Imperial Court. At one-and-twenty, in all the splendor of youth and beauty, Augustine saw herself deserted for a woman of six-and-thirty. Feeling herself so wretched in the midst of a world of festivity which to her was a blank, the poor little thing could no longer understand the admiration she excited, or the envy of which she was the object. Her face assumed a different expression. Melancholy, tinged her features with the sweetness of resignation and the pallor of scorned love. Ere long she too was courted by the most fascinating men; but she remained lonely and virtuous. Some contemptuous words which escaped her husband filled her with incredible despair. A sinister flash showed her the breaches which, as a result of her sordid education, hindered the perfect union of her soul with Theodore's; she loved him well enough to absolve him and condemn herself. She shed tears of blood, and perceived, too late, that there are mesalliances of the spirit as well as of rank and habits. As she recalled the early raptures of their union, she understood the full extent of that lost happiness, and accepted the conclusion that so rich a harvest of love was in itself a whole life, which only sorrow could pay for. At the same time, she loved too truly to lose all hope. At one-and-twenty she dared undertake to educate herself, and make her imagination, at least, worthy of that she admired. "If I am not a poet," thought she, "at any rate, I will understand poetry."

Then, with all the strength of will, all the energy which every woman can display when she loves, Madame de Sommervieux tried to alter her character, her manners, and her habits; but by dint of devouring books and learning undauntedly, she only succeeded in becoming less ignorant. Lightness of wit and the graces of conversation are a gift of nature, or the fruit of education begun in the cradle. She could appreciate music and enjoy it, but she could not sing with taste. She understood literature and the beauties of poetry, but it was too late to cultivate her refractory memory. She listened with pleasure to social conversation, but she could contribute nothing brilliant. Her religious notions and home-grown prejudices were antagonistic to the complete emancipation of her intelligence. Finally, a foregone conclusion against her had stolen into Theodore's mind, and this she could not conquer. The artist would laugh, at those who flattered him about his wife, and his irony had some foundation; he so overawed the pathetic young creature that, in his presence, or alone with him, she trembled. Hampered by her too eager desire to please, her wits and her knowledge vanished in one absorbing feeling. Even her fidelity vexed the unfaithful husband, who seemed to bid her do wrong by stigmatizing her virtue as insensibility. Augustine tried in vain to abdicate her reason, to yield to her husband's caprices and whims, to devote herself to the selfishness of his vanity. Her sacrifices bore no fruit. Perhaps they had both let the moment slip when souls may meet in comprehension. One day the young wife's too sensitive heart received one of those blows which so strain the bonds of feeling that they seem to be broken. She withdrew into solitude. But before long a fatal idea suggested to her to seek counsel and comfort in the bosom of her family.

So one morning she made her way towards the grotesque facade of the humble, silent home where she had spent her childhood. She sighed as she looked up at the sash-window, whence one day she had sent her first kiss to him who now shed as much sorrow as glory on her life. Nothing was changed in the cavern, where the drapery business had, however, started on a new life. Augustine's sister filled her mother's old place at the desk. The unhappy young woman met her brother-in-law with his pen behind his ear; he hardly listened to her, he was so full of business. The formidable symptoms of stock-taking were visible all round him; he begged her to excuse him. She was received coldly enough by her sister, who owed her a grudge. In fact, Augustine, in her finery, and stepping out of a handsome carriage, had never been to see her but when passing by. The wife of the prudent Lebas, imagining that want of money was the prime cause of this early call, tried to keep up a tone of reserve which more than once made Augustine smile. The painter's wife perceived that, apart from the cap and lappets, her mother had found in Virginie a successor who could uphold the ancient honor of the Cat and Racket. At breakfast she observed certain changes in the management of the house which did honor to Lebas' good sense; the assistants did not rise before dessert; they were allowed to talk, and the abundant meal spoke of ease without luxury. The fashionable woman found some tickets for a box at the Francais, where she remembered having seen her sister from time to time. Madame Lebas had a cashmere shawl over her shoulders, of which the value bore witness to her husband's generosity to her. In short, the couple were keeping pace with the times. During the two-thirds of the day she spent there, Augustine was touched to the heart by the equable happiness, devoid, to be sure, of all emotion, but equally free from storms, enjoyed by this well-matched couple. They had accepted life as a commercial enterprise, in which, above all, they must do credit to the business. Not finding any great love in her husband, Virginie had set to work to create it. Having by degrees learned to esteem and care for his wife, the time that his happiness had taken to germinate was to Joseph Lebas a guarantee of its durability. Hence, when Augustine plaintively set forth her painful position, she had to face the deluge of commonplace morality which the traditions of the Rue Saint-Denis furnished to her sister.

"The mischief is done, wife," said Joseph Lebas; "we must try to give our sister good advice." Then the clever tradesman ponderously analyzed the resources which law and custom might offer Augustine as a means of escape at this crisis; he ticketed every argument, so to speak, and arranged them in their degrees of weight under various categories, as though they were articles of merchandise of different qualities; then he put them in the scale, weighed them, and ended by showing the necessity for his sister-in-law's taking violent steps which could not satisfy the love she still had for her husband; and, indeed, the feeling had revived in all its strength when she heard Joseph Lebas speak of legal proceedings. Augustine thanked them, and returned home even more undecided than she had been before consulting

Honoré de Balzac

them. She now ventured to go to the house in the Rue
du Colombier, intending to confide her troubles to her
father and mother; for she was like a sick man who, in
his desperate plight, tries every prescription, and even
puts faith in old wives' remedies.

The old people received their daughter with an effu-
siveness that touched her deeply. Her visit brought them
some little change, and that to them was worth a fortune.
For the last four years they had gone their way like nav-
igators without a goal or a compass. Sitting by the chim-
ney corner, they would talk over their disasters under the
old law of maximum, of their great investments in cloth,
of the way they had weathered bankruptcies, and, above
all, the famous failure of Lecocq, Monsieur Guillaume's
battle of Marengo. Then, when they had exhausted the
tale of lawsuits, they recapitulated the sum total of their
most profitable stock-takings, and told each other old
stories of the Saint-Denis quarter. At two o'clock old
Guillaume went to cast an eye on the business at the
Cat and Racket; on his way back he called at all the
shops, formerly the rivals of his own, where the young
proprietors hoped to inveigle the old draper into some
risky discount, which, as was his wont, he never refused
point-blank. Two good Normandy horses were dying of
their own fat in the stables of the big house; Madame
Guillaume never used them but to drag her on Sundays
to high Mass at the parish church. Three times a week
the worthy couple kept open house. By the influence of
his son-in-law Sommervieux, Monsieur Guillaume had
been named a member of the consulting board for the
clothing of the Army. Since her husband had stood so
high in office, Madame Guillaume had decided that she
must receive; her rooms were so crammed with gold
and silver ornaments, and furniture, tasteless but of
undoubted value, that the simplest room in the house
looked like a chapel. Economy and expense seemed
to be struggling for the upper hand in every accessory.

It was as though Monsieur Guillaume had looked to a good investment, even in the purchase of a candlestick. In the midst of this bazaar, where splendor revealed the owner's want of occupation, Sommervieux's famous picture filled the place of honor, and in it Monsieur and Madame Guillaume found their chief consolation, turning their eyes, harnessed with eye-glasses, twenty times a day on this presentment of their past life, to them so active and amusing. The appearance of this mansion and these rooms, where everything had an aroma of staleness and mediocrity, the spectacle offered by these two beings, cast away, as it were, on a rock far from the world and the ideas which are life, startled Augustine; she could here contemplate the sequel of the scene of which the first part had struck her at the house of Lebas—a life of stir without movement, a mechanical and instinctive existence like that of the beaver; and then she felt an indefinable pride in her troubles, as she reflected that they had their source in eighteen months of such happiness as, in her eyes, was worth a thousand lives like this; its vacuity seemed to her horrible. However, she concealed this not very charitable feeling, and displayed for her parents her newly-acquired accomplishments of mind, and the ingratiating tenderness that love had revealed to her, disposing them to listen to her matrimonial grievances. Old people have a weakness for this kind of confidence. Madame Guillaume wanted to know the most trivial details of that alien life, which to her seemed almost fabulous. The travels of Baron da la Houtan, which she began again and again and never finished, told her nothing more unheard-of concerning the Canadian savages.

"What, child, your husband shuts himself into a room with naked women! And you are so simple as to believe that he draws them?"

As she uttered this exclamation, the grandmother laid her spectacles on a little work-table, shook her skirts,

49

and clasped her hands on her knees, raised by a foot-warmer, her favorite pedestal.

"But, mother, all artists are obliged to have models."

"He took good care not to tell us that when he asked leave to marry you. If I had known it, I would never had given my daughter to a man who followed such a trade. Religion forbids such horrors; they are immoral. And at what time of night do you say he comes home?"

"At one o'clock—two——"

The old folks looked at each other in utter amazement.

"Then he gambles?" said Monsieur Guillaume. "In my day only gamblers stayed out so late."

Augustine made a face that scorned the accusation.

"He must keep you up through dreadful nights waiting for him," said Madame Guillaume. "But you go to bed, don't you? And when he has lost, the wretch wakes you."

"No, mamma, on the contrary, he is sometimes in very good spirits. Not unfrequently, indeed, when it is fine, he suggests that I should get up and go into the woods."

"The woods! At that hour? Then have you such a small set of rooms that his bedroom and his sitting-room are not enough, and that he must run about? But it is just to give you cold that the wretch proposes such expeditions. He wants to get rid of you. Did one ever hear of a man settled in life, a well-behaved, quiet man galloping about like a warlock?"

"But, my dear mother, you do not understand that he must have excitement to fire his genius. He is fond of scenes which——"

"I would make scenes for him, fine scenes!" cried Madame Guillaume, interrupting her daughter. "How can you show any consideration to such a man? In the first place, I don't like his drinking water only; it is not wholesome. Why does he object to see a woman eating? What queer notion is that! But he is mad. All you tell us about him is impossible. A man cannot leave his home without a word, and never come back for ten days. And then he tells you he has been to Dieppe to paint the sea. As if any one painted the sea! He crams you with a pack of tales that are too absurd."

Augustine opened her lips to defend her husband; but Madame Guillaume enjoined silence with a wave of her hand, which she obeyed by a survival of habit, and her mother went on in harsh tones: "Don't talk to me about the man! He never set foot in church excepting to see you and to be married. People without religion are capable of anything. Did Guillaume ever dream of hiding anything from me, of spending three days without saying a word to me, and of chattering afterwards like a blind magpie?"

"My dear mother, you judge superior people too severely. If their ideas were the same as other folks', they would not be men of genius."

"Very well, then let men of genius stop at home and not get married. What! A man of genius is to make his wife miserable? And because he is a genius it is all right! Genius, genius! It is not so very clever to say black one minute and white the next, as he does, to interrupt other people, to dance such rigs at home, never to let you know which foot you are to stand on, to compel his wife never to be amused unless my lord is in gay spirits, and to be dull when he is dull."

"But, mother, the very nature of such imaginations——"

"What are such 'imaginations'?" Madame Guillaume went on, interrupting her daughter again. "Fine ones his are, my word! What possesses a man that all on a sudden, without consulting a doctor, he takes it into his head to eat nothing but vegetables? If indeed it were

from religious motives, it might do him some good—
but he has no more religion than a Huguenot. Was
there ever a man known who, like him, loved horses
better than his fellow-creatures, had his hair curled like
a heathen, laid statues under muslin coverlets, shut his
shutters in broad day to work by lamp-light? There, get
along; if he were not so grossly immoral, he would be fit
to shut up in a lunatic asylum. Consult Monsieur Loraux,
the priest at Saint Sulpice, ask his opinion about it all,
and he will tell you that your husband, does not behave
like a Christian."

"Oh, mother, can you believe——?"

"Yes, I do believe. You loved him, and you can see
none of these things. But I can remember in the early
days after your marriage. I met him in the Champs-Ely-
sees. He was on horseback. Well, at one minute he was
galloping as hard as he could tear, and then pulled up to
a walk. I said to myself at that moment, 'There is a man
devoid of judgement.'"

"Ah, ha!" cried Monsieur Guillaume, "how wise I was
to have your money settled on yourself with such a
queer fellow for a husband!"

When Augustine was so imprudent as to set forth
her serious grievances against her husband, the two
old people were speechless with indignation. But the
word "divorce" was ere long spoken by Madame Guillaume. At the sound of the word divorce the apathetic
old draper seemed to wake up. Prompted by his love
for his daughter, and also by the excitement which the
proceedings would bring into his uneventful life, father
Guillaume took up the matter. He made himself the
leader of the application for a divorce, laid down the
lines of it, almost argued the case; he offered to be at all
the charges, to see the lawyers, the pleaders, the judges,
to move heaven and earth. Madame de Sommervieux
was frightened, she refused her father's services, said

she would not be separated from her husband even if she were ten times as unhappy, and talked no more about her sorrows. After being overwhelmed by her parents with all the little wordless and consoling kindnesses by which the old couple tried in vain to make up to her for her distress of heart, Augustine went away, feeling the impossibility of making a superior mind intelligible to weak intellects. She had learned that a wife must hide from every one, even from her parents, woes for which it is so difficult to find sympathy. The storms and sufferings of the upper spheres are appreciated only by the lofty spirits who inhabit there. In any circumstance we can only be judged by our equals.

Thus poor Augustine found herself thrown back on the horror of her meditations, in the cold atmosphere of her home. Study was indifferent to her, since study had not brought her back her husband's heart. Initiated into the secret of these souls of fire, but bereft of their resources, she was compelled to share their sorrows without sharing their pleasures. She was disgusted with the world, which to her seemed mean and small as compared with the incidents of passion. In short, her life was a failure.

One evening an idea flashed upon her that lighted up her dark grief like a beam from heaven. Such an idea could never have smiled on a heart less pure, less virtuous than hers. She determined to go to the Duchesse de Carigliano, not to ask her to give her back her husband's heart, but to learn the arts by which it had been captured; to engage the interest of this haughty fine lady for the mother of her lover's children; to appeal to her and make her the instrument of her future happiness, since she was the cause of her present wretchedness.

So one day Augustine, timid as she was, but armed with supernatural courage, got into her carriage at two in the afternoon to try for admittance to the boudoir of the famous coquette, who was never visible till that hour. Madame de Sommervieux had not yet seen any of the ancient and magnificent mansions of the Faubourg Saint-Germain. As she made her way through the stately corridors, the handsome staircases, the vast drawing-rooms—full of flowers, though it was in the depth of winter, and decorated with the taste peculiar to women born to opulence or to the elegant habits of the aristocracy, Augustine felt a terrible clutch at her heart; she coveted the secrets of an elegance of which she had never had an idea; she breathed in an air of grandeur which explained the attraction of the house for her husband. When she reached the private rooms of the Duchess she was filled with jealousy and a sort of despair, as she admired the luxurious arrangement of the furniture, the draperies and the hangings. Here disorder was a grace, here luxury affected a certain contempt of splendor. The fragrance that floated in the warm air flattered the sense of smell without offending it. The accessories of the rooms were in harmony with a view, through plate-glass windows, of the lawns in a garden planted with evergreen trees. It was all bewitching, and the art of it was not perceptible. The whole spirit of the mistress of these rooms pervaded the drawing-room where Augustine awaited her. She tried to divine her rival's character from the aspect of the scattered objects; but there was here something as impenetrable in the disorder as in the symmetry, and to the simple-minded young wife all was a sealed letter. All that she could discern was that, as a woman, the Duchess was a superior person. Then a painful thought came over her.

"Alas! And is it true," she wondered, "that a simple and loving heart is not all-sufficient to an artist; that to balance the weight of these powerful souls they need a union with feminine souls of a strength equal to their own? If I had been brought up like this siren, our weapons at least might have been equal in the hour of struggle."

"But I am not at home!" The sharp, harsh words, though spoken in an undertone in the adjoining boudoir, were heard by Augustine, and her heart beat violently.

"The lady is in there," replied the maid.

"You are an idiot! Show her in," replied the Duchess, whose voice was sweeter, and had assumed the dulcet tones of politeness. She evidently now meant to be heard.

Augustine shyly entered the room. At the end of the dainty boudoir she saw the Duchess lounging luxuriously on an ottoman covered with brown velvet and placed in the centre of a sort of apse outlined by soft folds of white muslin over a yellow lining. Ornaments of gilt bronze, arranged with exquisite taste, enhanced this sort of dais, under which the Duchess reclined like a Greek statue. The dark hue of the velvet gave relief to every fascinating charm. A subdued light, friendly to her beauty, fell like a reflection rather than a direct illumination. A few rare flowers raised their perfumed heads from costly Sevres vases. At the moment when this picture was presented to Augustine's astonished eyes, she was approaching so noiselessly that she caught a glance from those of the enchantress. This look seemed to say to some one whom Augustine did not at first perceive, "Stay; you will see a pretty woman, and make her visit seem less of a bore."

On seeing Augustine, the Duchess rose and made her sit down by her.

"And to what do I owe the pleasure of this visit, madame?" she said with a most gracious smile.

"Why all the falseness?" thought Augustine, replying only with a bow.

Her silence was compulsory. The young woman saw before her a superfluous witness of the scene. This personage was, of all the Colonels in the army, the youngest, the most fashionable, and the finest man. His face, full of life and youth, but already expressive, was further enhanced by a small moustache twirled up into points, and as black as jet, by a full imperial, by whiskers carefully combed, and a forest of black hair in some disorder. He was whisking a riding whip with an air of ease and freedom which suited his self-satisfied expression and the elegance of his dress; the ribbons attached to his button-hole were carelessly tied, and he seemed to pride himself much more on his smart appearance than on his courage. Augustine looked at the Duchesse de Carigliano, and indicated the Colonel by a sidelong glance. All its mute appeal was understood.

"Good-bye, then, Monsieur d'Aiglemont, we shall meet in the Bois de Boulogne."

These words were spoken by the siren as though they were the result of an agreement made before Augustine's arrival, and she winged them with a threatening look that the officer deserved perhaps for the admiration he showed in gazing at the modest flower, which contrasted so well with the haughty Duchess. The young fop bowed in silence, turned on the heels of his boots, and gracefully quitted the boudoir. At this instant, Augustine, watching her rival, whose eyes seemed to follow the brilliant officer, detected in that glance a sentiment of which the transient expression is known to every woman. She perceived with the deepest anguish that her visit would be useless; this lady, full of artifice, was too greedy of homage not to have a ruthless heart.

"Madame," said Augustine in a broken voice, "the step I am about to take will seem to you very strange; but there is a madness of despair which ought to excuse anything. I understand only too well why Theodore prefers your house to any other, and why your mind has so much power over his. Alas! I have only to look into myself to find more than ample reasons. But I am devoted to my husband, madame. Two years of tears have not effaced his image from my heart, though I have lost his. In my folly I dared to dream of a contest with you; and I have come to you to ask you by what means I may triumph over yourself. Oh, madame," cried the young wife, ardently seizing the hand which her rival allowed her to hold, "I will never pray to God for my own happiness with so much fervor as I will beseech Him for yours, if you will help me to win back Sommervieux's regard—I will not say his love. I have no hope but in you. Ah! tell me how you could please him, and make him forget the first days——" At these words Augustine broke down, suffocated with sobs she could not suppress. Ashamed of her weakness, she hid her face in her handkerchief, which she bathed with tears.

"What a child you are, my dear little beauty!" said the Duchess, carried away by the novelty of such a scene, and touched, in spite of herself, at receiving such homage from the most perfect virtue perhaps in Paris. She took the young wife's handkerchief, and herself wiped the tears from her eyes, soothing her by a few monosyllables murmured with gracious compassion. After a moment's silence the Duchess, grasping poor Augustine's hands in both her own—hands that had a rare character of dignity and powerful beauty—said in a gentle and friendly voice: "My first warning is to advise you not to weep so bitterly; tears are disfiguring. We must learn to deal firmly with the sorrows that make us ill, for love does not linger long by a sick-bed. Melancholy, at first, no doubt, lends a certain attractive grace, but it ends by dragging the features and blighting the loveliest face. And besides, our tyrants are so vain as to insist that their slaves should be always cheerful."

"But, madame, it is not in my power not to feel. How is it possible, without suffering a thousand deaths, to see the face which once beamed with love and gladness turn chill, colorless, and indifferent? I cannot control my heart!"

57

"So much the worse, sweet child. But I fancy I know all your story. In the first place, if your husband is unfaithful to you, understand clearly that I am not his accomplice. If I was anxious to have him in my drawing-room, it was, I own, out of vanity; he was famous, and he went nowhere. I like you too much already to tell you all the mad things he has done for my sake. I will only reveal one, because it may perhaps help us to bring him back to you, and to punish him for the audacity of his behavior to me. He will end by compromising me. I know the world too well, my dear, to abandon myself to the discretion of a too superior man. You should know that one may allow them to court one, but marry them—that is a mistake! We women ought to admire men of genius, and delight in them as a spectacle, but as to living with them? Never.—No, no. It is like wanting to find pleasure in inspecting the machinery of the opera instead of sitting in a box to enjoy its brilliant illusions. But this misfortune has fallen on you, my poor child, has it not? Well, then, you must try to arm yourself against tyranny."

"Ah, madame, before coming in here, only seeing you as I came in, I already detected some arts of which I had no suspicion."

"Well, come and see me sometimes, and it will not be long before you have mastered the knowledge of these trifles, important, too, in their way. Outward things are, to fools, half of life; and in that matter more than one clever man is a fool, in spite of all his talent. But I dare wager you never could refuse your Theodore anything!"

"How refuse anything, madame, if one loves a man?"

"Poor innocent, I could adore you for your simplicity. You should know that the more we love the less we should allow a man, above all, a husband, to see the whole extent of our passion. The one who loves most is tyrannized over, and, which is worse, is sooner or later neglected. The one who wishes to rule should——"

"What, madame, must I then dissimulate, calculate, become false, form an artificial character, and live in it? How is it possible to live in such a way? Can you——" she hesitated; the Duchess smiled.

"My dear child," the great lady went on in a serious tone, "conjugal happiness has in all times been a speculation, a business demanding particular attention. If you persist in talking passion while I am talking marriage, we shall soon cease to understand each other. Listen to me," she went on, assuming a confidential tone. "I have been in the way of seeing some of the superior men of our day. Those who have married have for the most part chosen quite insignificant wives. Well, those wives governed them, as the Emperor governs us; and if they were not loved, they were at least respected. I like secrets—especially those which concern women—well enough to have amused myself by seeking the clue to the riddle. Well, my sweet child, those worthy women had the gift of analyzing their husbands' nature; instead of taking fright, like you, at their superiority, they very acutely noted the qualities they lacked, and either by possessing those qualities, or by feigning to possess them, they found means of making such a handsome display of them in their husbands' eyes that in the end they impressed them. Also, I must tell you, all these souls which appear so lofty have just a speck of madness in them, which we ought to know how to take advantage of. By firmly resolving to have the upper hand and never deviating from that aim, by bringing all our actions to bear on it, all our ideas, our cajolery, we subjugate these eminently capricious natures, which, by the very mutability of their thoughts, lend us the means of influencing them."

"Good heavens!" cried the young wife in dismay. "And this is life. It is a warfare——"

"In which we must always threaten," said the Duchess, laughing. "Our power is wholly factitious. And we must never allow a man to despise us; it is impossible to recover from such a descent but by odious manoeuvring. Come," she added, "I will give you a means of bringing your husband to his senses."

She rose with a smile to guide the young and guileless apprentice to conjugal arts through the labyrinth of her palace. They came to a back-staircase, which led up to the reception rooms. As Madame de Carigliano pressed the secret springlock of the door she stopped, looking at Augustine with an inimitable gleam of shrewdness and grace. "The Duc de Carigliano adores me," said she. "Well, he dare not enter by this door without my leave. And he is a man in the habit of commanding thousands of soldiers. He knows how to face a battery, but before me,—he is afraid!"

Augustine sighed. They entered a sumptuous gallery, where the painter's wife was led by the Duchess up to the portrait painted by Theodore of Mademoiselle Guillaume. On seeing it, Augustine uttered a cry.

"I knew it was no longer in my house," she said, "but—here!——"

"My dear child, I asked for it merely to see what pitch of idiocy a man of genius may attain to. Sooner or later I should have returned it to you, for I never expected the pleasure of seeing the original here face to face with the copy. While we finish our conversation I will have it carried down to your carriage. And if, armed with such a talisman, you are not your husband's mistress for a hundred years, you are not a woman, and you deserve your fate."

Augustine kissed the Duchess' hand, and the lady clasped her to her heart, with all the more tenderness because she would forget her by the morrow. This scene might perhaps have destroyed for ever the candor and purity of a less virtuous woman than Augustine, for the astute politics of the higher social spheres were no more consonant to Augustine than the narrow reasoning of Joseph Lebas, or Madame Guillaume's vapid morality. Strange are the results of the false positions into which we may be brought by the slightest mistake in the conduct of life! Augustine was like an Alpine cowherd surprised by an avalanche; if he hesitates, if he listens to the shouts of his comrades, he is almost certainly lost. In such a crisis the heart steels itself or breaks.

Madame de Sommervieux returned home a prey to such agitation as it is difficult to describe. Her conversation with the Duchesse de Carigliano had roused in her mind a crowd of contradictory thoughts. Like the sheep in the fable, full of courage in the wolf's absence, she preached to herself, and laid down admirable plans of conduct; she devised a thousand coquettish stratagems; she even talked to her husband, finding, away from him, all the springs of true eloquence which never desert a woman; then, as she pictured to herself Theodore's clear and steadfast gaze, she began to quake. When she asked whether monsieur were at home her voice shook. On learning that he would not be in to dinner, she felt an unaccountable thrill of joy. Like a criminal who has appealed against sentence of death, a respite, however short, seemed to her a lifetime. She placed the portrait in her room, and waited for her husband in all the agonies of hope. That this venture must decide her future life, she felt too keenly not to shiver at every sound, even the low ticking of the clock, which seemed to aggravate her terrors by doling them out to her. She tried to cheat time by various devices. The idea struck her of dressing in a way which would make her exactly like the portrait. Then, knowing her husband's restless temper, she had her room lighted up with unusual brightness, feeling sure that when he came in curiosity would bring him there at once. Midnight had struck when, at the call of the groom, the street gate was opened, and the artist's carriage rumbled in over the stones of the silent courtyard.

"What is the meaning of this illumination?" asked Theodore in glad tones, as he came into her room.

Augustine skilfully seized the auspicious moment; she threw herself into her husband's arms, and pointed to the portrait. The artist stood rigid as a rock, and his eyes turned alternately on Augustine, on the accusing dress. The frightened wife, half-dead, as she watched her husband's changeful brow—that terrible brow—saw the expressive furrows gathering like clouds; then she felt her blood curdling in her veins when, with a glaring look, and in a deep hollow voice, he began to question her:

"Where did you find that picture?"

"The Duchess de Carigliano returned it to me."

"You asked her for it?"

"I did not know that she had it."

The gentleness, or rather the exquisite sweetness of this angel's voice, might have touched a cannibal, but not an artist in the clutches of wounded vanity.

"It is worthy of her!" exclaimed the painter in a voice of thunder. "I will be avenged!" he cried, striding up and down the room. "She shall die of shame; I will paint her! Yes, I will paint her as Messalina stealing out at night from the palace of Claudius."

"Theodore!" said a faint voice.

"I will kill her!"

"My dear——"

"She is in love with that little cavalry colonel, because he rides well——"

"Theodore!"

"Let me be!" said the painter in a tone almost like a roar.

It would be odious to describe the whole scene. In the end the frenzy of passion prompted the artist to acts and words which any woman not so young as Augustine would have ascribed to madness.

At eight o'clock next morning Madame Guillaume, surprising her daughter, found her pale, with red eyes, her hair in disorder, holding a handkerchief soaked with tears, while she gazed at the floor strewn with the torn fragments of a dress and the broken fragments of a large gilt picture-frame. Augustine, almost senseless with grief, pointed to the wreck with a gesture of deep despair.

"I don't know that the loss is very great!" cried the old mistress of the Cat and Racket. "It was like you, no doubt; but I am told that there is a man on the boulevard who paints lovely portraits for fifty crowns."

"Oh, mother!"

"Poor child, you are quite right," replied Madame Guillaume, who misinterpreted the expression of her daughter's glance at her. "True, my child, no one ever can love you as fondly as a mother. My darling, I guess it all; but confide your sorrows to me, and I will comfort you. Did I not tell you long ago that the man was mad! Your maid has told me pretty stories. Why, he must be a perfect monster!"

Augustine laid a finger on her white lips, as if to implore a moment's silence. During this dreadful night misery had led her to that patient resignation which in mothers and loving wives transcends in its effects all human energy, and perhaps reveals in the heart of women the existence of certain chords which God has withheld from men.

An inscription engraved on a broken column in the cemetery at Montmartre states that Madame de Sommervieux died at the age of twenty-seven. In the simple words of this epitaph one of the timid creature's friends can read the last scene of a tragedy. Every year, on the second of November, the solemn day of the dead, he never passes this youthful monument without wondering whether it does not need a stronger woman than Augustine to endure the violent embrace of genius?

"The humble and modest flowers that bloom in the valley," he reflects, "perish perhaps when they are transplanted too near the skies, to the region where storms gather and the sun is scorching."

www.ingramcontent.com/pod-product-compliance
Lightning Source LLC
Chambersburg PA
CBHW021937170626
46807CB00007B/3164